2.00

SECRET OF THE PEACEFUL WARRIOR

A Story About Courage and Love

Dan Millman
author of
Way of the Peaceful Warrior

Illustrated by
T. Taylor Bruce

H J Kramer Inc
Starseed Press
Tiburon, California

To my daughters,
Sierra and China.
And to children everywhere.
D.M.

In gratitude
to my mother and father,
for all of the beauty
with which they surrounded me.
T.T.B.

On a crisp morning in autumn, in a town not far
away, Danny Morgan sat gazing out the kitchen window
at his new neighborhood. Gone were the familiar back-
yard and his old friends. Today was his first day at
Eastside School. Part of him was excited; another part
was afraid.

From the next room, his mother called out, "Finish
your breakfast, Danny! The neighbor's boy will be here
any minute to walk with you to school."

The doorbell rang. As Danny dumped the remains of his oatmeal in the sink, his mother handed him a new lunch box. The doorbell rang again. "Well?" she said, smiling. "Are you going to open the door?"

In the doorway Danny saw a girl about his age. "My name is Joy," she said.

Turning toward his mother, Danny whispered, "Ma, you said it was going to be a *boy*!"

"I thought they said *Joe*," she whispered back. Louder, she added, "Have a good time, honey —see you after school," and gave him a big kiss.

Blushing, Danny wiped the kiss off his face, turned to Joy, and said with a sigh, "Okay, let's go."

They walked past Baker's Pond, past a row of old houses, and across the railroad tracks when, suddenly, Carl Brady, the school bully, stepped out from behind a parked car and blocked their path.

Danny tried to walk around him, but the older boy reached out and grabbed Danny's lunch box, tore it open, and looked inside. Disgusted, he threw the box on the ground scattering the contents over the sidewalk. He turned to Danny and snarled, "Where's your money?"

Danny reached into his pocket and slowly took out a five-dollar bill—his spending money for the whole week.

The older boy held out his hand. As Danny pulled the crinkled bill out of his pocket, they were startled by a voice behind them. "*Don't give it to him, Danny!*"

They turned to see Joy with her hands on her hips. "*I* have money," she said to the bully, "and it's yours if you catch me—but you're so slow, you couldn't even catch a cold!"

Both boys gaped at her, hardly believing her nerve.

"*What?*" Danny whispered.

"*WHAT?*" Carl bellowed. His face grew red. He clenched his fists. Then he lunged at Joy.

She just laughed, dodged him, and ran toward school. Carl took off after her, but she was too fast for him.

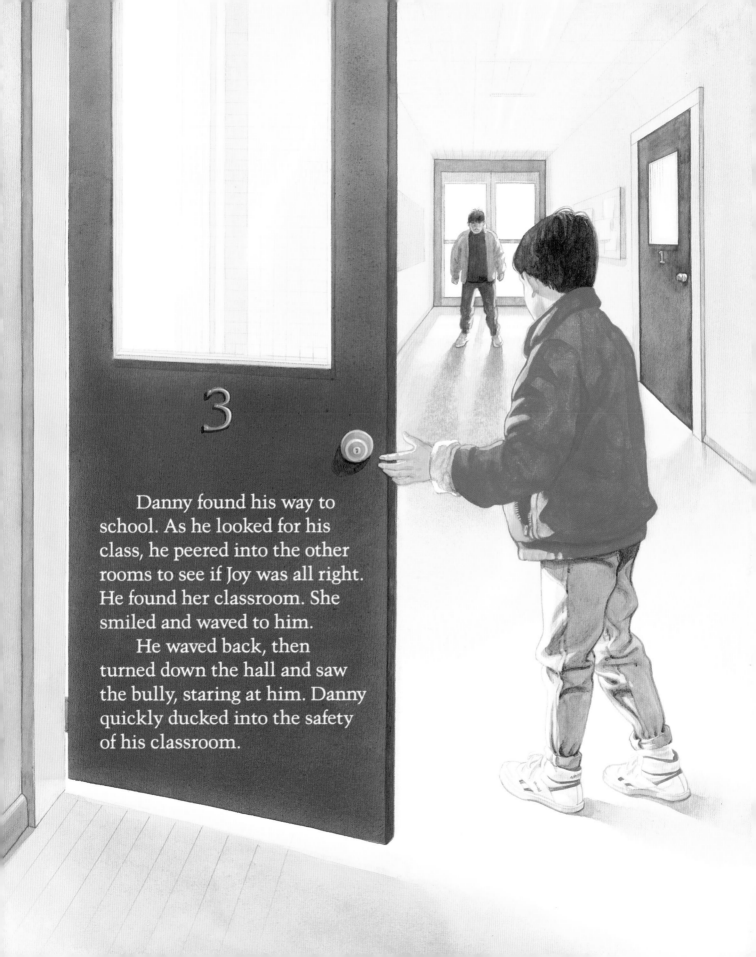

Danny found his way to school. As he looked for his class, he peered into the other rooms to see if Joy was all right. He found her classroom. She smiled and waved to him.

He waved back, then turned down the hall and saw the bully, staring at him. Danny quickly ducked into the safety of his classroom.

At lunch, Danny found Joy, sitting on the lawn, opening her lunch. "Thanks for what you did," he said.

"That's okay," she answered, holding out half of her sandwich. "I guess you're hungry. Want some?"

He nodded and took the sandwich from her. As they ate, he looked out across the school yard and saw the bully shooting baskets by himself. "He used to have a few friends," Joy said. "Then his father ran off, and his mother left him with an uncle or somebody like that. Since then, he's always alone. Everybody's afraid of him."

"Except you," Danny said.

"I can outrun him," Joy smiled.

"How'd you learn to run so fast?" Danny asked.

"My grandfather taught me."

Danny hesitated, then asked, "Do you think he could teach me, too?"

Joy shrugged. "I don't know. You could ask him. He lives over there," she said, pointing to an old house across the street. "He's a gardener," she added. "His name is Socrates."

That night, as Danny drifted off to sleep, he found himself in a dark cave. Something was chasing him. Frightened, he tried to run, but could hardly move—it was like running through thick molasses.

He could see an opening in the cave, filled with sunlight, but the exit was blocked by a huge, dark shape.

Danny felt someone else nearby. He turned and
saw an old man with white hair, reaching out to him.
"Who are you?" Danny asked.
The old man only smiled.
Danny woke up. It was morning.

The next day at school, Danny managed to avoid the bully during lunch. But after school, Carl spotted Danny and started toward him.

Danny quickly crossed the street, but the older boy was closing in. In a panic, he ran up some steps and pounded on a door. Then he realized it was where Joy's grandfather lived.

The door opened. Danny gasped as he saw, in the doorway, the old man from his dream!

The old man smiled at Danny, then down at Carl, waiting below. "I'm Socrates," he said. "I guess you're Danny."

"How—how did you know my name?" Danny stammered.

Instead of answering, Socrates handed Danny a bushel basket. "I'm going to pick a few apples in the front yard. I could use some help."

Glancing back toward Carl, Danny decided to follow the old man into the safety of his yard.

Socrates climbed a ladder and started to pick the crisp red apples, tossing them one by one to Danny, who put them into the basket.

"Uh, Mr. Socrates . . ." Danny began.

"Not 'mister,'" the old man interrupted. "Just Socrates. And you can call me 'Soc.'"

Danny nodded. "Well, . . . Soc, could you teach me to run as fast as Joy?"

Socrates paused, then bit into one of the crunchy apples, and tossed another to Danny. "You know, this tree is about your age. I've taken care of it for nine years . . . helped it to grow into a strong, healthy apple tree. But I can't change it into an orange tree."

"I don't understand," Danny said.

"I didn't *change* Joy into a fast runner," Soc replied. "She already had that ability inside her; I just helped her to bring it out. You have other gifts."

"But I *have* to learn to run! That boy's after me. You saw him."

"Yes, I understand. But if you run from a problem, even if you get away for a while, it keeps chasing you," Socrates said as he sat on the ladder and tossed more apples to Danny. "The best way to escape from a problem, my young friend, is to solve it."

"How can I solve it?" Danny asked, putting the apples into the basket.

"When you're no longer afraid of him, he'll stop."

"But I *am* afraid!"

Socrates climbed down the ladder and said, "The secret of courage is to act brave even if you're not feeling very brave."

"How can I do that?" Danny asked, looking down at the ground.

Socrates climbed down the ladder. "Have you ever pretended to be someone else?"

Danny thought for a moment: "I was a wizard once . . . in a school play."

Socrates placed his hand on Danny's shoulder and looked into his eyes. "If you can be a wizard . . . you can be a warrior."

"But I don't know *how* to be a warrior."

"You didn't know how to tie your shoes once, either."

"I'll tell you what," Soc said, pointing to a spot on the lawn. "If you can show me how to do a forward handspring, I'll show you how to be a warrior."

"I've never done a handspring."

"That's what I thought," Soc replied. "But try it anyway."

Doubtful, Danny lifted his arms, threw himself forward onto his hands, kicked wildly around, and fell down. "I *told* you I didn't know how!" he grumbled.

"Again!" Socrates said, grinning. "But this time, keep your arms straight and your head back."

Danny tried and fell again. But he kept trying, and each time he got a little closer.

Suddenly, to his surprise, Danny found himself standing up balanced on his feet. "I did it!" he yelled.

"Yes! And that's *exactly* how you learn courage, or anything else," Soc explained. "It may not be easy at first, but keep practicing. You'll get it."

After that, Danny visited Socrates every day—
careful to avoid Carl on the way. One day, while helping
Soc in his garden, Danny asked, "How can I ever fight
him? He's bigger than I am and stronger."

Socrates paused, then went into the garage and
pulled out an old wagon. "I have to deliver a plant to
someone up on Scenic Hill. Think you could pull this
wagon all the way to the top?"

"Sure I can," Danny answered quickly.
But he didn't know that Socrates was going
to be *in* the wagon.

As Danny struggled up the grade,
breathing hard, he asked, "Can we stop
for a minute? This is really hard!"

"Sometimes *life* is an uphill struggle, just like this hill," Socrates observed. "Other times, it feels easy, like coasting downhill."

"I wish it was *all* downhill," Danny said, panting.

"Coasting down *is* easier," Soc replied. "But which makes you stronger?"

Danny smiled. "I understand," he said, wiping his brow as they reached the top of the grade.

They delivered the plant, and sat in the wagon poised at the top of the hill, when Socrates added, "Another thing about life, Danny— if you don't make the climb *up*, you never get to enjoy the ride *down*." Then Soc pushed off, and down they flew!

Every day after that, Danny pulled Socrates up the hill as they made deliveries. Danny's muscles ached in places he didn't even know he had muscles. But he was feeling stronger than ever before.

A few days later, as Danny struggled to pull Socrates up, a woman in her front yard scowled at Soc and said, "You ought to be ashamed of yourself, you lazy old man!"

Danny laughed so hard he almost let go of the wagon.

In Soc's garden the next day Danny flexed a new muscle and slammed his fist into his palm. "Just let that Carl try to push me around again! He'll be sorry!"

Socrates stopped when he heard this, and frowned. He turned to Danny and challenged, "I'll give you five dollars if you can push me off balance."

"Really?" Danny asked.

"Really," Soc answered.

"Okay then," Danny yelled. "You asked for it!" He lunged at Socrates. A moment later, Danny found himself flat on his back on the lawn.

"How did you do that?" he asked.

Socrates looked at him a long time before answering: "You'll understand that when you can do it yourself."

Soc stood in front of Danny. "Go ahead now—push me again."

Danny lunged again, but at the last second, Soc stepped out of the way, took Danny's arm, and with a gentle pull, threw him to the grass.

Socrates reached down to help Danny up. "You *are* getting strong—but there's always going to be someone stronger. I once told you that running isn't the answer; well, neither is fighting. If you hurt someone else, it only makes *you* the bully. The true warrior is a *peaceful* warrior."

"But . . . what if someone attacks me first?"

"No one has a right to hurt you, Danny. You have a right to defend yourself."

"But—how can I defend myself without hurting someone else?" asked Danny.

Socrates pointed to a small tree, bending in the wind. "That tree knows the warrior's secret," he said. "If it resists, it may break. So it bends with the force.

"Never resist someone's force, Danny; use it. If they pull, you push. If they push, you pull. And remember—if a railroad train is coming your way, get off the tracks! Deal with whatever happens this way, and your life will be easier."

"Okay," Danny said. "Try to push *me* this time!"

For the next few weeks, Danny practiced "getting off the tracks." It wasn't as easy as it looked, but he'd learned the value of practice, and one day he sent Socrates sprawling. This time it was Danny's turn to help Socrates up.

Socrates smiled, "Danny—I think you've got it." Danny hugged Soc, and ran home like the wind!

The next day, as Danny and Joy were walking home from school, he saw Carl, waiting ahead in the shadow of a tree. Danny stopped for a moment and took a deep breath. Looking straight ahead, he continued on his way.

Carl stepped in front of Danny. "You're not gonna hide behind a girl this time!" he threatened.

Danny's heart was pounding, but he kept walking. "Don't run and don't fight," he reminded himself.

Carl hesitated, puzzled by Danny's confidence. Then he yelled, "Stop right there!" and reached out to seize Danny's arm.

Just as Carl grabbed him,
Danny stepped out of the way and gave
a small tug on the older boy's sleeve.
Off balance, Carl stumbled forward,
and fell. Furious, he jumped up and lunged again.

Once more Danny evaded him, and Carl fell again. This time,
he didn't get up. He just sat there, staring at the ground.

In that moment, Danny knew that Carl would never bother
him again. Then he realized something even more important. Carl
had never really been his enemy. Fear had been his opponent all
the time. He had faced the fear, and conquered it. His battle was
over.

Danny turned back, walked up to the older boy, and offered
him a hand. Carl only turned away, ashamed. He got up and
walked away, sad and defeated.

The next day at lunchtime, it was very hot. Danny
was standing in line to buy a lemonade when he saw
Carl off to the side, staring at the cold drinks. Danny
guessed that Carl had no money.

When Danny reached the front of the line, he
slapped down a dollar on the counter. "One lemonade,
for me, please," he said. "And a lemonade for my friend,"
he added, nodding toward Carl.

Many feelings passed across the older boy's face.
Carl hesitated, then reached out to take the juice. He
started to say something, but couldn't find the right
words—so he just nodded and turned away. For the first
time, Danny understood how lonely he must be.

A few days later after school, Danny saw Carl shooting baskets—alone as usual. Danny approached, took a deep breath, and spoke: "You really have a good hook shot. I've never been able to do one."

Carl stopped shooting. He gazed at Danny, but his attention was deep inside himself, as if deciding something important. Finally, with difficulty, he spoke. "A hook shot isn't hard—just takes a little practice. Come here, I'll show you."

Joy was just leaving her class when she saw them playing. She watched from a distance for a while, then approached. "Could I play?"

Carl stopped shooting. He glared at her, and said nothing. Then his face softened into a smile. "Sure," he said, throwing her the ball. "Any friend of Danny Morgan is a friend of mine."

That night, Danny's dreams took him again into a dark cave. Socrates was nowhere in sight, only the shadow figure, blocking the way out. But this time, it wasn't so big. And this time Danny knew the secret:

He didn't run. He didn't fight. He faced it squarely, his arms open wide, and walked toward the light at the end of the tunnel. And as he passed through the dark shape of fear, it became transparent, glittered for a moment, then vanished, because no fear can withstand the courage, and love, of the peaceful warrior.

Danny Morgan woke up smiling. He watched his curtains billow in the fresh morning breeze. Outside, a sparrow flew up into the sky. And there, shining through his window, was the light of the new day.

All children are seeds from the stars who look to adults for love, inspiration, guidance, and the promise of a safe and friendly world. We dedicate Starseed Press to this vision and to the sacred child in each of us.

Hal and Linda Kramer,
Publishers

H J Kramer Inc
P.O. Box 1082
Tiburon, CA 94920

Library of Congress Cataloging-in-Publication Data

Millman, Dan.
    Secret of the peaceful warrior: a children's story about courage and love / Dan Millman; illustrated by T. Taylor Bruce.
        p.   cm.
    "A book to help children grow."
    Summary: An old man named Socrates shows Danny that the best way of dealing with a bully is the way of the peaceful warrior, through courage and love.
    ISBN 0-915811-23-5
    [1. Courage—Fiction.   2. Bullies—Fiction.   3. Conduct of life—Fiction.]   I. Bruce, T. Taylor, ill. II. Title.
    PZ7.M6395Se   1991
    [E]—dc20   90-52636
                                                                       CIP
                                                                        AC

Editor: Robert San Souci
Art Director: Linda Kramer
Editorial Assistant: Nancy Grimley Carleton
Book Production: Schuettge and Carleton
Typography: Metrotype & Communication Arts
Printed in Singapore
10 9 8 7 6 5 4 3